GREAT FAIRY TALE CLASSICS

ILLUSTRATED BY PIERO CATTANEO
TEXT BY PETER HOLEINONE

© DAMI EDITORE, ITALY

Published by Tormont Publications Inc.
338 Saint Antoine St. E.
Montreal, Quebec
CANADA H2Y IA3

Printed in Italy

Printed by Officine Grafiche De Agostini S.p.A.
Bound by Legatoria del Verbano S.p.A.

The story of

LITTLE RED
RIDING HOOD

and other tales

Once upon a time . . .

. . . a big bad wolf was roaming hungrily through a great forest. One day, he saw a basket covered with a white cloth lying on the ground, and his greedy eyes peered around . . .

LITTLE RED RIDING HOOD

Once upon a time . . . in the middle of a thick forest stood a small cottage, the home of a pretty little girl known to everyone as Little Red Riding Hood. One day, her Mummy waved her goodbye at the garden gate, saying: "Grandma is ill. Take her this basket of cakes, but be very careful. Keep to the path through the wood and don't ever stop. That way, you will come to no harm."

Little Red Riding Hood kissed her mother and ran off. "Don't worry,' she said, "I'll run all the way to Grandma's without stopping."

Full of good intentions, the little girl made her way through the wood, but she was soon to forget her mother's wise words. "What lovely strawberries! And so red . . ."

Laying her basket on the ground, Little Red Riding Hood bent over the strawberry plants. "They're nice and ripe, and so big! Yummy! Delicious! Just another one. And one more. This is the last . . . Well, *this* one . . . Mmmm."

The red fruit peeped invitingly through the leaves in the grassy glade, and Little Red Riding Hood ran back and forth popping strawberries into her mouth. Suddenly she remembered her mother, her promise, Grandma and the basket . . . and hurried back towards the path. The basket was still in the grass and, humming to herself, Little Red Riding Hood walked on.

The wood became thicker and thicker. Suddenly a yellow butterfly fluttered down through the trees. Little Red Riding Hood started to chase the butterfly.

"I'll catch you! I'll catch you!" she called. Suddenly she saw some large daisies in the grass.

"Oh, how sweet!" she exclaimed and, thinking of Grandma, she picked a large bunch of flowers.

In the meantime, two wicked eyes were spying on her from behind a tree . . a strange rustling in the woods made Little Red Riding Hood's heart thump.

Now quite afraid, she said to herself, "I must find the path and run away from here!"

At last, she reached the path again, but her heart leapt into her mouth at the sound of a gruff voice which said: "Where are you going, my pretty girl, all alone in the woods?"

"I'm taking Grandma some cakes. She lives at the end of the path," said Little Riding Hood in a faint voice.

When he heard this, the wolf (for it was the big bad wolf himself) politely asked: "Does Grandma live by herself?"

"Oh, yes," replied Little Red Riding Hood, "and she never opens the door to strangers!"

"Goodbye. Perhaps we'll meet again," replied the wolf. Then he loped away thinking to himself "I'll gobble the grandmother first, then lie in wait for the grandchild!" At last, the cottage came in sight. Knock! Knock! The wolf rapped on the door.

"Who's there?" cried Grandma from her bed.

"It's me, Little Red Riding Hood. I've brought you some cakes because you're ill," replied the wolf, trying hard to hide his gruff voice.

"Lift the latch and come in," said Grandma, unaware of anything amiss, till a horrible shadow appeared on the wall. Poor Grandma! For in one bound, the wolf leapt across the room and, in a single mouthful, swallowed the old lady. Soon after, Little Red Riding Hood tapped on the door.

"Grandma, can I come in?" she called.

Now, the wolf had put on the old lady's shawl and cap and slipped into the bed. Trying to imitate Grandma's quavering little voice, he replied: "Open the latch and come in!"

"What a deep voice you have," said the little girl in surprise.

"The better to greet you with," said the wolf.

"Goodness, what big eyes you have."

"The better to see you with."

"And what big hands you have!" exclaimed Little Red Riding Hood, stepping over to the bed.

"The better to hug you with," said the wolf.

"What a big mouth you have," the little girl murmured in a weak voice.

"The better to eat you with!" growled the wolf, and jumping out of bed, he swallowed her up too. Then, with a fat full tummy, he fell fast asleep.

In the meanwhile, a hunter had emerged from the wood, and on noticing the cottage, he decided to stop and ask for a drink. He had spent a lot of time trying to catch a large wolf that had been terrorising the neighbourhood, but had lost its tracks. The hunter could hear a strange whistling sound; it seemed to be coming from inside the cottage. He peered through the window . . . and saw the large wolf himself, with a fat full tummy, snoring away in Grandma's bed.

"The wolf! He won't get away this time!"

Without making a sound, the hunter carefully loaded his gun and gently opened the window. He pointed the barrel straight at the wolf's head and . . . BANG! The wolf was dead.

"Got you at last!" shouted the hunter in glee. "You'll never frighten anyone again."

He cut open the wolf's stomach and to his amazement, out popped Grandma and Little Red Riding Hood, safe and unharmed.

"You arrived just in time," murmured the old lady, quite overcome by all the excitement.

"It's safe to go home now," the hunter told Little Red Riding Hood. "The big bad wolf is dead and gone, and there is no danger on the path."

Still scared, the little girl hugged her grandmother. "Oh, what a dreadful fright!"

Much later, as dusk was falling, Little Red Riding Hood's mother arrived, all out of breath, worried because her little girl had not come home. And when she saw Little Red Riding Hood, safe and sound, she burst into tears of joy.

After thanking the hunter again, Little Red Riding Hood and her mother set off towards the wood. As they walked quickly through the trees, the little girl told her mother: "We must always keep to the path and never stop. That way, we'll come to no harm!"

THE MAGIC TINDERBOX

Once upon a time . . . a brave soldier returned from the wars. In spite of his courage, his pockets were empty and his only possession was his sword. As he walked through a forest, he met a witch, who said to him: "I say, good soldier, would you like to earn a bag of money?"

"Money? I'd do anything for money . . ."

"Good!" went on the witch. "It won't be difficult, you'll see! All you have to do is go down that hollow tree till you reach a cave. There, you'll find three doorways. When you open the first door, you'll see a big dog with eyes like saucers, guarding a large chest of copper coins. Behind the second door lies a treasure of silver coins, guarded by a dog with eyes the size of mill stones. When you open the third door, you'll come upon another dog, with eyes the size of a castle tower, beside a treasure of gold. Now, if you lay this old apron of mine before these dogs, they'll crouch on it and do you no harm. You'll be able to carry away all the coins you want. What do think of that?"

However, the soldier suspiciously asked: "What do you want in return?"

"Just bring me back an old tinderbox my grandfather left down there, long ago!"

So the young soldier tied a rope round his waist and, not forgetting his trusty sword, he lowered himself into the hollow tree. To his great surprise, he found the three doorways and the three dogs, just as the witch had said. Soon he was back, his pockets bulging with coins, but before he handed the tinderbox to the old witch, he asked her: "What do you want it for?"

The witch hurled herself at the soldier, screaming: "Give it to me! Give it to me at once, or else . . .", as she tried to scratch him. When the witch attacked him, the soldier exclaimed: "Aha! So this is the thanks I get! Now I'll show *you*!"

He undid the rope from around his waist and tied up the old woman. Then away he went, whistling cheerfully.

When he reached the town, he said to himself: "Now I can feast as much as I like – at last!"

After years of scrimping on a miserable pay, with his sudden wealth, the soldier felt like a prince. He bought a new pair of boots and he went to the best tailor in the town. Some days later, he was clad in a fine new uniform and people turned in the street to admire him. Lavish with his money, the soldier was surrounded by folk quick to tell him how to spend his coins, and it all went on a round of dances, fine carriages, theatres and, most of all, on drinking sprees. Of course, his money soon ran out and when this happened, his "friends" vanished. When the innkeeper discovered that the soldier could no longer pay his board, he rudely put him out. So the poor soldier ended up in a garret and every day he had to draw in his belt a little more. All the fun was over.

One evening, he realised he had never used the old witch's tinderbox. So he rubbed it, and as it sparked, the dog with the eyes like saucers suddenly appeared.

"Tell me your wish, sir," it said.

". . . bring me heaps of money!" gasped the soldier in amazement. A second later, the dog was back with a bag of coins. Every time he rubbed the tinderbox, the dog brought him more money. Then when he rubbed it quickly twice in succession, the dog with eyes like mill stones stood before him, carrying silver coins. And when the soldier rubbed the tinderbox three times in a row, the third dog came carrying gold. Rich all over again, the soldier chose the best hotel in the town and went back to leading the life of a fine gentleman.

The soldier was told that the King would not allow anyone

to meet his beautiful daughter, for he believed in a saying that the Princess's destiny was to marry a simple soldier. That evening, the soldier rubbed the tinderbox. "Bring me the Princess," was his new order. Immediately the dog returned with the beautiful Princess, fast asleep. The soldier kissed her. Next morning, the girl told her parents that she had had a dream. But the Queen, suspiciously ordered one of the ladies-in-waiting to guard her daughter day and night. The dog was seen when it came next evening and the alarm raised. The king's guards followed the dog and the soldier was arrested at dawn.

The King's revenge was terrible: the soldier was to be hanged!

In a dark prison, the soldier calmly awaited his fate. When the day of execution came, a mob crushed round the scaffold.

The soldier asked if he could smoke his pipe, and placed it between his lips, as he rubbed the tinderbox over and over again. In a flash, the three dogs appeared with gaping jaws and bloodshot eyes. At the soldier's sharp command, they leapt on the guards and the crowd cheered in delight.

Awestruck at this magic feat, the King bowed his head and whispered to the Queen. "The saying is true!" he said. A little while after, the young soldier married the Princess and the tinderbox was rubbed and rubbed, but this time to invite the three dogs to the splendid wedding.

THE LITTLE MATCHGIRL

Once upon a time . . . a little girl tried to make a living by selling matches in the street.

It was New Year's Eve and the snowclad streets were deserted. From brightly lit windows came the tinkle of laughter and the sound of singing. People were getting ready to bring in the New Year. But the poor little matchseller sat sadly beside the fountain. Her ragged dress and worn shawl did not keep out the cold and she tried to keep her bare feet from touching the frozen ground. She hadn't sold one box of matches all day and she was frightened to go home, for her father would certainly be angry. It wouldn't be much warmer anyway, in the draughty attic that was her home. The little girl's fingers were stiff with cold. If only she could light a match! But what would her father say at such a waste! Falteringly she took out a match and lit it. What a nice warm flame! The little matchseller cupped her hand over it, and as she did so, she magically saw in its light a big brightly burning stove.

She held out her hands to the heat, but just then the match went out and the vision faded. The night seemed blacker than before and it was getting colder. A shiver ran through the little girl's thin body.

After hesitating for a long time, she struck another match on the wall, and this time, the glimmer turned the wall into a great sheet of crystal. Beyond that stood a fine table laden with food and lit by a candlestick. Holding out her arms towards the plates, the little matchseller seemed to pass through the glass, but then the match went out and the magic faded. Poor thing: in just a few seconds she had caught a glimpse of everything that life had denied her: warmth and good things to eat. Her eyes filled with tears and she lifted her gaze to the lit windows, praying that she too might know a little of such happiness.

She lit the third match and an even more wonderful thing happened. There stood a Christmas tree hung with hundreds of candles, glittering with tinsel and coloured balls. "Oh, how lovely!" exclaimed the little matchseller, holding up the match. Then, the match burned her finger and flickered out. The light from the Christmas candles rose higher and higher, then one of the lights fell, leaving a trail behind it. "Someone is dying," murmured the little girl, as she remembered her beloved Granny who used to say: "When a star falls, a heart stops beating!"

Scarcely aware of what she was doing, the little matchseller lit another match. This time, she saw her grandmother.

"Granny, stay with me!" she pleaded, as she lit one match after the other, so that her grandmother could not disappear like all the other visions. However, Granny did not vanish, but gazed smilingly at her. Then she opened her arms and the little girl hugged her crying: "Granny, take me away with you!"

A cold day dawned and a pale sun shone on the fountain and the icy road. Close by lay the lifeless body of a little girl surrounded by spent matches.

"Poor little thing!" exclaimed the passersby. "She was trying to keep warm!"

But by that time, the little matchseller was far away where there is neither cold, hunger nor pain.

THE PIED PIPER OF HAMELIN

Once upon a time . . . on the banks of a great river in the north of Germany lay a town called Hamelin. The citizens of Hamelin were honest folk who lived contentedly in their grey stone houses. The years went by, and the town grew very rich. Then one day, an extraordinary thing happened to disturb the peace. Hamelin had always had rats, and a lot too. But they had never been a danger, for the cats had always solved the rat problem in the usual way – by killing them. All at once, however, the rats began to multiply.

In the end, a black sea of rats swarmed over the whole town. First, they attacked the barns and storehouses, then, for lack of anything better, they gnawed the wood, cloth or anything at all. The one thing they didn't eat was metal. The terrified citizens flocked to plead with the town councillors to free them from the plague of rats. But the council had, for a long time, been sitting in the Mayor's room, trying to think of a plan.

"What we need is an army of cats!"

But all the cats were dead.

"We'll put down poisoned food then . . ."

But most of the food was already gone and even poison did not stop the rats.

"It just can't be done without help!" said the Mayor sadly.

Just then, while the citizens milled around outside, there was a loud knock at the door. "Who can that be?" the city fathers wondered uneasily, mindful of the angry crowds. They gingerly opened the door. And to their surprise, there stood a tall thin man dressed in brightly coloured clothes, with a long feather in his hat, and waving a gold pipe at them.

"I've freed other towns of beetles and bats," the stranger announced, "and for a thousand florins, I'll rid you of your rats!"

"A thousand florins!" exclaimed the Mayor. "We'll give you *fifty thousand* if you succeed!" At once the stranger hurried away, saying: "It's late now, but at dawn tomorrow, there won't be a rat left in Hamelin!"

The sun was still below the horizon, when the sound of a pipe wafted through the streets of Hamelin. The pied piper slowly made his way through the houses and behind him flocked the rats. Out they scampered from doors, windows and gutters, rats of every size, all after the piper. And as he played, the stranger marched down to the river and straight into the water, up to his middle. Behind him swarmed the rats and every one was drowned and swept away by the current.

By the time the sun was high in the sky, there was not a single rat in the town. There was even greater delight at the town hall, until the piper tried to claim his payment.

"Fifty thousand florins?" exclaimed the councillors, "Never . . ."

" A thousand florins at least!" cried the pied piper angrily. But the Mayor broke in. "The rats are all dead now and they can never come back. So be grateful for fifty florins, or you'll not get even that . . ."

His eyes flashing with rage, the pied piper pointed a threatening finger at the Mayor.

"You'll bitterly regret ever breaking your promise," he said, and vanished.

A shiver of fear ran through the councillors, but the Mayor shrugged and said excitedly: "We've saved fifty thousand florins!"

That night, freed from the nightmare of the rats, the citizens of Hamelin slept more soundly than ever. And when the strange sound of piping wafted through the streets at dawn, only the children heard it. Drawn as by magic, they hurried out of their homes. Again, the pied piper paced through the town, but this time, it was children of all sizes that flocked at his heels to the sound of his strange piping. The long procession soon left the town and made its way through the wood and across the forest till it reached the foot of a huge mountain. When the piper came to the dark rock, he played his pipe even louder still and a great door creaked open.

Beyond lay a cave. In trooped the children behind the pied piper, and when the last child had gone into the darkness, the door creaked shut. A great landslide came down the mountain blocking the entrance to the cave forever. Only one little lame boy escaped this fate. It was he who told the anxious citizens, searching for their children, what had happened. And no matter what people did, the mountain never gave up its victims. Many years were to pass before the merry voices of other children would ring through the streets of Hamelin but the memory of the harsh lesson lingered in everyone's heart and was passed down from father to son through the centuries.

THE SNOW QUEEN

Once upon a time . . . a magician made a magic mirror. In this mirror, a kind face became wicked, a look of hate was reflected as a look of love. One day, however, the mirror broke, and if a sliver of glass from the mirror entered someone's eye, that person's soul became evil, if another pierced a heart, that heart grew hard and cold as ice.

In a big town, two children, called Karl and Gerda were very close friends, and even the sweet pea that grew on Karl's window sill spread across the street to entwine with Gerda's little rose bush. One evening Karl was watching the snow drift down, when he noticed a white flake slowly turn into a beautiful ice maiden. Karl was startled to hear the ice maiden speak his name, and he was not to know he had set eyes on the Snow Queen. Winter passed, and one spring afternoon, as Karl and Gerda pored over a book, the little boy told her: "I feel a pain in my heart! And something's pricking my eye!"

"Don't worry," said Gerda comfortingly. "I can't see anything!" But, alas, splinters from the shattered mirror had pierced the little boy.

Now in the grip of the evil spell, he snapped: "You're so ugly!" And ripping two roses from her bush, he ran off. From that day on, Karl turned into a very nasty boy, and nobody could understand what had happened to him to cause such a change. Only Gerda still loved him, though all she got in return were insults and spite.

Winter came round again, though earlier than usual, and bringing far more snow than anyone could remember.

One day, just after going outdoors to play in the snow, Karl saw the beautiful maiden he had seen that night, coming towards him wrapped in a white fur coat. She stood in front of him and told him to tie his sledge to her own, drawn by a white horse. Then they sped away. Suddenly, the great sledge soared into the sky and through the clouds. Stretched out on his own little sledge, Karl didn't dare move a muscle for fear of falling into space. At last, they came to a halt on an immense white plain, dotted with lots of sparkling frozen lakes.

"Come into my arms," said the Snow Queen, opening her soft fur coat. "Come and keep warm!"

Karl allowed himself to be hugged by the unknown maiden and a chill ran up his spine as two icy lips touched his forehead. The Snow Queen kissed him again, and in an instant, the little boy forgot all about Gerda and his past life, as he fell into a deep sleep.

In the meanwhile, Gerda was anxiously searching for Karl, but no-one had seen him. Finally, she went down to the river.

"Great river," she said, "please tell me if you've seen Karl or if you've carried him away! I'll give you these, if you do!" And she threw her shoes into the river. But the current paid no heed and just swept them back to the bank. Not far away stood an old boat, and Gerda climbed into it. As she drifted with the current, she pleaded: "Great river, silently flowing and knowing all things about men's lives, take me to Karl."

At dusk, she stopped by a river bank carpeted with all kinds of flowers. After resting she went into the forest, and though she did not know how she would ever find her friend, a mysterious voice inside her told her to be brave. After wandering far and wide, she stopped, tired and hungry. A crow flapped out from a hollow tree.

"If you're looking for Karl," it said, "I know where he is! I saw him with the Snow Queen on her sledge in the sky!"

"And where is her kingdom?" Gerda asked the crow.

"In Lapland, where all is icy cold. That reindeer over there might take you!"

Gerda ran over to the big reindeer, threw her arms around its neck and, laying her cheek against its soft muzzle, said: "Please help me to find my friend!"
The reindeer's kindly eyes told her that he would, and she

climbed onto its back. They travelled till they came to the frozen tundra, lit by the fiery glow of the Northern Lights.

"Karl! Karl! Where are you?" shouted Gerda as loudly as she could. When, at last, she found the little boy, Karl did not recognise her. Gerda threw her arms round him, and teardrops dripped on to his chest and heart. This broke the evil spell. Karl woke from his long sleep, and when he set eyes on Gerda, he too began to cry. The second cold splinter of mirror vanished. They had found each other again at last, thanks to Gerda's love, and the reindeer galloped them home. The two plants on the window sills started to blossom again and to twine, a sign of their everlasting friendship.

THE POPLAR AND THE STREAM

Once upon a time . . . a woodcutter called Ivan lived in a huge forest in the north of Russia. A sturdy young man, with his bare hands he built himself a stout log cabin and when it was finished, he thought he would look for a wife. His dream was of a beautiful maiden, tall, slender and fair, with blue eyes and a creamy skin.

On Sundays he roamed to distant villages looking for the girl of his dreams. But the only girls he ever saw were dull and not pretty enough.

As it so happened, the path he took to work passed close to a pretty little house with green shutters. Often, the corner of a curtain would be raised and a sweet-faced girl would watch the woodcutter as he went by. For he had unwittingly lit the flames of love in a maiden's heart. This young girl was called Natasha; she was very shy, but her love for the woodcutter was so great that, one day, she plucked up enough courage to stop him on the path.

"I picked this basket of strawberries myself," she said. "Please eat them and think of me!"

"Well, she's not exactly ugly," said Ivan to himself as he stared woodenly at Natasha, who was blushing to the roots of her hair.

"I don't like strawberries," he replied bluntly. "But thanks all the same!"

Tears sprang to Natasha's eyes as she watched him stride away. A few days later, the girl again stopped Ivan and held out a woollen jacket, saying: "The air will be chilly tonight when you go home. This will keep you warm. I made it myself."

But Ivan coldly replied: "What makes you think that a man like me is afraid of the cold?"

And this time, at Ivan's refusal, two tears rolled down Natasha's rosy cheeks and she fled sobbing into the house.

However, Natasha again watched for the woodcutter. This time, she held out a bottle and said: "You can't refuse a liqueur that I distilled from all the fruits of the forest! It will . . ." But Ivan broke in saying: "I don't like liqueurs," and marched straight on. However, he realised he had been very rude, so he turned round, but Natasha had gone. As he walked, he said to himself: " She has gentle eyes . . . and she must be very kind-hearted! Perhaps I should take at least one of her gifts, but . . ."
The picture of his dream girl slipped into his mind. "I'm so unhappy!" he sighed.

At that very moment, on a golden cloud appeared a beautiful lady. "Will you sing a song for me? I'm Rosalka, one of the woodland fairies!" Ivan stood thunderstruck.

"I'd sing for you for the rest of my life!" he exclaimed, "If only I could . . ." and he stretched out his hand to touch the fairy, but she floated out of reach amongst the branches.

"Sing then! Sing! Only the sound of your voice will ever send me to sleep!" So Ivan happily sang all the old lullabies and love songs, while the drowsy fairy urged him on: "Sing! Sing!"

Cold and weary, his voice getting hoarser the woodcutter sang till evening, as he tried to help the fairy to fall asleep. But when night fell, Rosalka was still demanding: "If you love me, sing on! Sing!"

As the woodcutter sang on, in a feeble voice, he kept thinking: "I wish I had a jacket to keep me warm!"

Suddenly he remembered Natasha.

"What a fool I am!" he told himself. "I should have chosen her as my bride, not this woman who asks and gives nothing in return!"

Ivan felt that only the gentle-faced Natasha could fill his empty heart. He fled into the darkness, but he heard a cruel voice call: ". . . you'll never see her again! All her tears for her great love have turned her into a stream! You'll never see her again!"

It was dawn when Ivan knocked at Natasha's door. No-one answered. And the woodcutter saw, with fear, that close by flowed a tiny sparkling stream he had never noticed before. Weeping sorrowfully, he plunged his face into the water.

"Oh, Natasha, how could I have been so blind! And I love you now!" Lifting his gaze to the sky, he silently said a prayer: "Let me stay beside her forever!"

Ivan was magically turned into a young poplar tree and the stream bathed its roots. Natasha had, at last, her beloved Ivan by her side for ever.

THE LITTLE GOLDEN BIRD

Once upon a time . . . several Buddhist monks lived in a great temple that stood in a magnificent garden full of flowers and rare plants. The monks spent their days contentedly in prayer and meditation, and the beauty of their surroundings was all they needed to make them forget the world. Then one day, something happened to change their life in this peaceful corner, making the days seem shorter and not so monotonous. No longer did they live peacefully together, indeed they started to quarrel. But what had happened?

A young monk had arrived, upsetting their lives by telling them all about the outside world beyond the garden wall. He told them about cities, the bright lights, everyday life full of entertainments and pleasure. And when the monks heard about this different world, they no longer wanted to remain in what had, till then, seemed paradise, but now turned into a lonely existence.

With the young monk as their leader, first one group then another left the temple. Weeds began to sprout on the paths and the temple was almost deserted. Then the last five monks, torn between their love for the sacred spot and the wish to see the new world they'd heard about, sadly got ready to leave.

But just as they were about to turn their backs on the temple, a golden bird, dangling five long white strings, fluttered over their heads. Each monk felt himself drawn to clasp one of the strings, and suddenly the little group found itself carried away to the land of their dreams. And there, they saw the outside world as it really was, full of hate, misery and violence, a world without scruples, where peace was forever banned.

It was a long journey, and when the golden bird brought them back to the temple garden, they decided never to leave it again. Three times the bird circled overhead before it vanished into the sky. And the monks knew then that Buddha had come to help them find the pathway to true happiness.

NARCISSUS

Once upon a time . . . in Ancient Greece lived a young man called Narcissus, who was greatly admired, for he was very handsome. Narcissus was very proud of his perfect face and graceful body, and never lost the chance to look at his reflection in any sheet of water he happened to pass. He would lie for hours admiring his gleaming dark eyes, slender nose, slim hips and the mop of curly hair that crowned the perfect oval of his face. You would think a sculptor had come down from heaven to carve such a faultless body as a living image of mankind's love of beauty.

One day, Narcissus was walking close to a precipice where the clear waters of a cold mountain pool mirrored his beautiful face.

"You *are* handsome, Narcissus!" he told himself as he bent down to admire his reflection. "There's nobody so handsome in the whole world! I'd love to kiss you."

Narcissus was suddenly seized by the desire to kiss his own reflection and he leant closer to the water. But he lost his balance and toppled into the pool. Narcissus could not swim and so he drowned. But when the gods discovered that the most beautiful being on earth had died, they decided that such beauty could not be forgotten.

The gods turned Narcissus into a scented flower which, to this day, blossoms in the mountains in spring, and which is still called Narcissus.

THE RUBY PRINCE

Once upon a time . . . a beggar in faraway Persia had a stroke of luck. After a sudden flood, the fast-flowing river near the capital city shrank back to its old bed, leaving mud and slime behind it on the banks. In the dirt, the beggar caught sight of a sparkling red stone. He picked it up and hurried off to visit one of his friends who worked in the royal kitchens.

"How many dinners would you give me for this shining stone?" he asked the man hopefully.

"But this is a ruby!" exclaimed the cook. "You must take it to the Shah at once!" So next day, the beggar took the stone to the Shah, who asked him: "Where did you find this?"

"Lying in the mud on the bank of the river, Sire!" he said.

"Hmm!" mused the Shah. "Now why did the great river leave such a treasure to *you*? I'll give you a bag of gold for the stone. Will that do?" The beggar could scarcely believe his ears.

"Sire, this is the most wonderful day of my life," he stammered. "My humblest thanks!"

Before the Shah locked the big stone in his treasure box, he called Fatima, his daughter and said: "This is the biggest ruby I've ever seen. I shall give it to you for your 18th birthday!"

Fatima admired the gem in her hand and happily threw her arms round her father's neck.

"It's marvellous! Thank you so much. I know it will bring me good luck!"

Some months later, on Fatima's birthday, the Shah went to fetch the ruby as promised. But when he lifted the lid of the box, he leapt in surprise, for out stepped a handsome young man, who smilingly said, "The ruby you want no longer exists! I've taken its place. I'm the Ruby Prince. Please don't ask me how this miracle took place. It's a secret I can never tell!"

When the Shah got over his shock, he went into a towering rage. "I lose a precious gem, find a prince, and I'm not allowed to ask the reason why?" he roared.

"I'm sorry, Sire," replied the prince, "but nothing and nobody will make me tell how I got here."

Furious at these words, the Shah instantly decided to punish the young man for his impertinence.

"Since you've taken the place of my ruby," he thundered, "you are now my servant, I presume."

"Of course, Sire," replied the young man confidently.

"Good!" exclaimed the Shah. "Then take my gold sword. I'll reward you with the hand of my daughter Fatima if you succeed in killing the dragon of Death Valley that's stopping the caravans from passing through the forest."

As it happens, many a brave young man had lost his life trying to kill the terrible dragon, and the Shah was quite sure that the Ruby Prince would share their fate.

Armed with the Shah's sword, the Ruby Prince set off for Death Valley. When he reached the edge of the thick dark forest, he loudly called for the dragon to show itself. But the only reply was the echo of his own voice. He leant against a tree trunk and was about to drop off to sleep when the sound of snapping branches brought him to his feet. A frightful hissing grew louder and louder and the earth trembled. The terrible dragon was on its way.

Before him the huge horrible beast reared with open jaws. Unlike all the other brave warriors who had gone before him, the prince stoutly stood his ground; he took a step forward and struck first one heavy blow at the dragon's throat, then another, till at last the monster lay dead at his feet.

When he returned to the palace carrying the dragon's head, the Ruby Prince was hailed as a hero. And so Fatima and the Ruby Prince were married and lived happily together. However, as time passed, Fatima became more and more curious about her husband's past.

"I know nothing about you," she complained. "At least tell me who you really are and where you once lived!"

But every time the Ruby Prince heard such remarks, he went white and said, "I can't tell you. You mustn't ask, or you'll run the risk of losing me for ever!"

But Fatima was tormented by the desire to know. One day, as they sat by the river that flowed through the Shah's gardens, Fatima pleaded with him to reveal his secret.

White-faced, the young man replied, "I can't!"

But Fatima only pleaded more: "Oh, please! Please tell me!"

"You know I can't . . ."

The Ruby Prince hesitated, gazing at his dearly loved wife and gently stroking her hair. Then he made his decision.

"I don't want to see you suffer like this. If you really must know, then I'll tell you that I'm . . ."

At the very second he was about to reveal his secret, a huge wave swept him into the river and dragged him under the water.

The horrified Princess rushed vainly along the bank, crying loudly for her husband. But he had vanished. Fatima called the guards and even the Shah himself ran up to comfort her. But the Princess became very depressed, for she knew that her foolish questioning had been the cause of the tragedy. One day, her favourite handmaiden hurried up to her.

"Your Highness!" she exclaimed. "I saw the most amazing thing last night. A host of tiny lights appeared on the river, then a thousand little genies draped the river bank with flowers. Such a handsome young man then began to dance in honour of an old man who seemed to be a king. And beside the king stood a young man with a ruby on his forehead. I thought he was . . ."

Fatima's heart leapt: could the young man with the ruby be her husband?

That night, the Princess and her handmaiden went into the garden and hid behind a tree close to the water's edge. On the stroke of midnight, tiny lights began to twinkle on the river, then a stately old man with a white beard, dressed in a golden robe and holding a sceptre, rose from the water.

In the young man beside the throne, Fatima recognised her husband. Covering her face with her veil, she left her hiding place and gracefully began to dance. Wild applause greeted her at the end. Then from the throne came a voice.

"For such a divine dance, ask us whatever you wish for and it will be granted!"

Fatima tore the veil from her face and cried, "Give me back my husband!"

The old king rose to his feet. "The King of the Waters of Persia gave his word. Take back your husband, the Ruby Prince. But do not forget how you lost him and be wiser in future!"

Then the waters opened once more and closed over the King and his Court, leaving Fatima and the Ruby Prince on the bank, reunited and happy at last.